SOME DADDIES

by Carol Gordon Ekster

illustrated by Javiera Mac-lean Álvarez

beaming books

MINNEAPOLIS

Text copyright © 2022 Carol Gordon Ekster
Illustrations by Javiera Mac-lean Álvarez, copyright © 2022 Beaming Books

28 27 26 25 24 23 22   1 2 3 4 5 6 7 8 9

Hardcover ISBN: 978-1-5064-6056-7
eBook ISBN: 978-1-5064-6886-0

Library of Congress Cataloging-in-Publication Data

Names: Ekster, Carol Gordon, author. | Mac-lean Álvarez, Javiera,
    illustrator.
Title: Some daddies / by Carol Gordon Ekster ; illustrated by Javiera
    Mac-lean Álvarez.
Description: Minneapolis, MN : Beaming Books, [2022] | Audience: Ages 5-8.
    | Summary: Illustrations and text celebrate fathers of all shapes,
    sizes, personalities, and interests.
Identifiers: LCCN 2021026515 (print) | LCCN 2021026516 (ebook) | ISBN
    9781506460567 (hardcover) | ISBN 9781506468860 (ebook)
Subjects: CYAC: Fathers--Fiction. | LCGFT: Picture books.
Classification: LCC PZ7.E3478 So 2022 (print) | LCC PZ7.E3478 (ebook) |
    DDC [E]--dc23
LC record available at https://lccn.loc.gov/2021026515
LC ebook record available at https://lccn.loc.gov/2021026516

VN0004589; 9781506460567; APR2022

Beaming Books
PO Box 1209
Minneapolis, MN 55440-1209
Beamingbooks.com

With gratitude to my humble, generous, sweet, wonderful father, Sidney Gordon, whose bright light let others shine. He asked for little and gave greatly. I miss him so!

And to my much-loved grandson, Aziah, who planted the seed for this story.

—C.G.E.

For my beloved husband, Walter, who fills our little son Oliver with color, patience, and wisdom.

The best father in the world.

—J.M.A.

Every daddy is different.

Some daddies wake up whistling.

Others need time before they talk.

Some joke around and tell stories.

Others like to listen.

Some daddies blend fruit smoothies.

Others sip steaming coffee or tea.

Some chug a mug of milk.

Others fill water bottles.

Some daddies dress in suits.

Others put on
protective gear
or uniforms.

Some work from home . . . in pajamas!

Others wear comfy clothes to care for you.

Every daddy is different.

Some daddies grow scratchy stubble.

Others choose soft skin and a smooth chin.

Some hide their lips
with a fancy mustache.

Others' beards drop
down to their bellies!

Some daddies shoot hoops.

Others hike woodsy trails dense with the smell of pine.

Some ski the slopes.

Others glide along
city streets.

Some daddies create art.

Others prune plants.

Some putter about.

Others spend time
reading . . . or napping!

*Every daddy
is different.*

Some daddies teach you about the world.

Others attend tea parties.

Some help turn blankets into forts.

Others hold you steady while you pedal.

Some daddies push you high . . .
then higher!

Others toss balls . . .
to you and the dog!

Some hold their arms out
to catch you. *Oops!*

Every daddy makes mistakes.
(*Every* human does.)

Some daddies share comforting words and cry with you.

Others love making you laugh.

Some barely hug.

Others hug like bears!

*Every daddy
is different.*

Some whip up meals from scratch.

Others prefer to grill.

Some dish out delivery.

Others dine without you,
wishing you were there.

Some daddies tuck you in with a song.

Others, with a book or two.

Some, with a snuggle.

Others, with a funny-faced goodnight.

Some daddies are yours from the time you are born.

Others are favorite grown-ups, chosen for a special day . . . or all your life.

CELEBRATING DADS

Some pick you.
Some you pick.

Others share you
with another daddy.

It's absolutely true . . .

. . . every daddy is different.

Every child is, too!

ABOUT THE AUTHOR

CAROL GORDON EKSTER is a children's book author and retired elementary school teacher. She is the author of *Where Am I Sleeping Tonight?: Kids Coming to Terms with Divorce*, *Ruth the Sleuth and the Messy Room*, *Before I Sleep I Say Thank You*, and *You Know What?*. She hopes her books help children navigate through life. She lives in Andover, Massachusetts.

ABOUT THE ILLUSTRATOR

JAVIERA MAC-LEAN ÁLVAREZ is a Chilean children's book illustrator who likes to use illustration as a voice to raise awareness for making a better world.